Simply Living Is Art

Collected Poems 1999 - 2018

Matthew Lotti

ISBN-10: 0-9715594-6-5
ISBN-13: 978-0-9715594-6-2

Cover photograph of the Baltic Sea by Theresa Lotti.

Contents

Demimonde

1999

Dedicated to the memory of Mark Rothko

"Woman is not born: she is made. In the making, her humanity is destroyed. She becomes symbol of this, symbol of that: mother of the earth, slut of the universe; but she never becomes herself because it is forbidden for her to do so."

- Andrea Dworkin

"For my part I distrust all generalizations about women, favorable and unfavorable, masculine and feminine, ancient and modern; all alike, I should say, result from paucity of experience."

- Bertrand Russell

Chicago

city with the starshine
three days without a break
a park outside congestion
a street beside a lake

pacing, frantic languor
with its intake absolute
pan of poisoned redness
in mass of seething brute

salt fumes in a vacuum
tunnels in the air
depression triggers sadness
but we could hardly care

dead in lasting coma
spiritual midnight trance
hanging from the meat hooks
for our celestial dance

a drive to western fleeting
we return on the same path
three livers full of fever
and the commonplace's wrath

Song From the Voice of an Unknown in Southern California

it's so good to see
you both in this town
with Mom all made up
like a rodeo clown
and you in your dress shirt
and I in my Chaps
and Felix, the feline
in a ball in your lap

just the other night
my friend Jake and I
snuck into the Skybar
behind the blind guy
we saw Julia Stiles
full of vigor and bile
she asked for a smoke
and forgot she should smile

worked with Pacino
he laughed quite a lot
kept socks in his shoes
and champagne in his cot
Cameron wouldn't look at
her own deli tray
too tired from tinkering
with brown modeling clay

I spend most of my life
screwing with sound
from the mouths of the people
with their heads in the ground
who talk about Jesus and

Buddha and crying
but not about cum
or why beggars are dying

it's hard to be hip
when the stones slide away
from the feet in the ground
in the heat of the day
in the rooms with the lights
and the beds with the milk
and the blood from the fights
on the sheets made of silk

but don't worry Dad
I still feel quite tall
I jumped off the Strip
but never could fall

Untitled

25 million people
blink in unison
at least once
in a while
(statistically)

Untitled

He senses still the stolid
but pays for it with pain
and fears the breath tomorrow
with its diagnostic name
he strengthens muscles clearly
with steel in molded form
and sees the others sweating
with flesh all red and warm

Untitled

I am indebted to those who stood by me, and who talked to me, and created the illusion of care. I'm not troubled if it really was an illusion. At least they bothered to put on the act in the first place.

or

I am indebted to those who stood by me, and who talked to me, and created the illusion of care. I'm not troubled if it really was an illusion. Because if they genuinely felt caring, I'm not sure I could handle it.

Untitled

A twenty-one-year-old
with a two-year-old
is married to a nineteen-year-old,
son of a forty-year-old,
and a thirty-nine-year-old,
brother of someone dead.

The twenty-one-year-old
plays with the two-year-old
and treats the nineteen-year-old
as if she were a nineteen-year-old
who acts like a six-year-old
and unfortunately for the two-year-old,
this can never work.

Wintertime

mystified little skater
finds friends beneath the ground
who talk a moving whisper
and never make a sound
they do it very slowly
keeping caution second thought
while pantomiming snow flakes
fall gracefully on the lot

Untitled

I admit
I'm not your king
and you're not my queen
but what's wrong with that?

well,
my mind told me a lie
it said I had style:
just maintain your poise
and develop a smile

but
I never did try
to give a hello
or mention goodbye

now
can't get you out of my heart
off of my page
your flowing white blouse
and unblemished face

I
stay away from the phone
since you're never there
and it's only this country
that we'll ever share

Return

a saturnine ending
to a saturday dance
your conscience was quiet
so you gave it a chance

provoked by the dawn
and her infinite sight
to soothe the faint impulse
to leave out of spite

she said she can not
abide by your dream
she thought you were sweet
though not what you seem

your lies are a burden
you're average at best
the sidewalk is calling
so please go get dressed

Demimonde

Rail-thin Russian waitress
with all-consuming eyes
stops us with a shuffle
and melts us with her sighs

shiny, classic statues
are never quite exact
their makers never think how
their little figures crack

she spends the night with refuse
who demand a tiny share
she'll please the male inside them
and never seem to care

she arises with the silence
and rediscovers clothes
she finds her strength in coffee
and some powder for her nose

redemption won't come quickly
only sadness fills its place
'Don't take me,' she implores us
before tending to our waste

Untitled

hopeful nymphs slithering to princely states
bow in servitude to those enjoying their dance
and contempt for those who prefer
a pillow
to a floor

Untitled

Where are you
my snide, literate darling?
Have you been away?
Are you well?
No matter: you can stay away -
this I have no problem with -
but kindly ask a thought
for me.
A thought:
a chemical shudder.
That is all.
I will continue to think of your well-being.

Big Ben on the Night I Can't Remember

shiver (panic) the grass bleeds gray
dew sparkles shimmers shines today
fog lifts enlightens punctures breeds
while trees from coastlines spill their seeds

pint and pint and pint of zest
my elbows grace cloth covered breast
the manual told me it's a wily test
to pass alone and without much rest

a landmark constructed for its own sake!
no sand but neurons, no dust but flake!
i've seen souls in the drifting, love in the past
and the union jack at permanent half-mast

the river of dreams is somewhere nearby
the pills in my palm could get me that high
oh freezing wind, to you i surrender
and your pulsating tower that i'll never remember

Advice

Our peers, friends, family tell us the same thing: forget about her, move on, there are many others like her out there, you need to stop this brooding, this nonsense. But these people are all wrong. There are other women, but the other women are not her. She is unique, complete, self-contained - to infer otherwise would imply that everyone is the same, that selectivity is irrelevant. Strides may be made to branch out, to find other links, to move forward, but nothing will ever be the same. The memory, infallible as it is, retains.

Untitled

some people with their free time
never stop to think
about the modes that others take
that send them to the brink
they never mingle with the lost souls
or crumble with the good
or tussle with the banshees
although they feel they could
they own no stock in freedom
but sing the air divine
they peddle petty afterthoughts
and suggest you walk the line

Untitled

it was one of the those moments
that will never leave me completely
beautiful
in how it affected all of me -
both of us,
in the same area
of the same room
completely and totally alone
(everyone else asleep)
me sitting reading a pamphlet
on sociology
you watching/listening
to a program on the set
wearing headphones
fidgeting for some natural reason
your chair
turned facing away -
it was the only chance
to approach
with mock bravado
and to trudge away
perhaps silent
but knowing
nonetheless.

(reticence does more harm
than good)

Hikikomori

lepers stealing fingers
lawyers selling smart
pacifying blankets
give life a friendly start

but should your patience falter
and you tire of the mess
fire off that mental rocket
and forget that wedding dress

hide out in your bedroom
make friends with quiet muck
avoid incessant staring
curse your horrid luck

dream the dream of gypsies
watch a moving show
play a violent nightmare
enjoy the TV glow

huddle with your comrades
give The Man a spiteful shrug
if you need a dollar
become the local thug

schooling is for nothing
work steals away your time
communication's worthless
and freedom is a crime

Advertisement for a Gardener

To be perfect for my job
it would be a pleasure if the
following demands were met:

The hedges in the garden
spread wildly like the ebony inkblots
and their wild patterns, with leaves
growing here, twigs there, and to
tend to their needs periodically
would be a blessing and minimize
the yard's irritation.

Shaping them would be the wisest of choices -
into shapes like squares or triangles -
because this is the most appealing to the eye,
a machine that is exacting and unforgiving
with regards to what makes it glad.

Be wary not to remove them entirely,
as this is a disaster for the pulsating
energy and the life of the yard: barren, young,
undeveloped - this should only appeal to those
without moderate, refined sensibilities.

The hedges require chemical care aside from
the pruning and attention - use of sprays and
other liquids is adequate - to keep ruthless
invaders from nestling and burrowing, causing
diseases and rotting, from the decay reeking
of contamination and poison, from overdeveloping
and grinding deeper into dry, nutrient-deprived soil.

The space between one hedge and another ought
to be as small as possible -
tight, narrow - because unhealthy, worn hedges
spreading apart unchecked suggest unabashed
recklessness and a lack of genuine concern for
the modern aesthetic.

Experience is a plus (as well as
willingness to experiment with alternative
forms of treatment) but not 'excessive'
experience, I should add, for one should
never know everything and forever
be willing to learn more.

Untitled

Tremors of silent rage
rattle inside me
every single moment
of every startling morning.
These sensations suggest
that I give up the quest
and resign to the fact
that it is not going to be simple
and that connections
will have
to be lost.

Untitled

do you have the problem I do
or do I remain alone
with a paper full of pixels
where thoughts are free to roam
do these persecutions wager
in your cloudy walking breeze
or are all these plagues unseemly
and ushered northward as you please?

Untitled

Carbon-copy mistress
from a block along the way
said all could be forgiven
in the span of just one day
but she never dared to mention
or even give the thought
that all your failure's waiting
for peril can't be fought.

Untitled

Tenderness in waste.
The concept is so foreign.
Anything that isn't perfect
(for you, of course)
is all the more repellent
and to be mostly ignored

Untitled

Be ever wary
of the woman
you marry
she'll leave you
one night
with all the change
she can carry
Those nights out alone:
to "just have a laugh?"
Her trip's not to mother, fool,
you do the math.

Mission Beach

I'm watching festive patter
(not a friendly sight)
and some buzzards
in all their richness
are circling the seascape.
Sadly,
people are still swimming
and the waves are not consuming -
I show a look
of disgust
when they return
to their blankets
alive.

Advice

smile, son. keep your
eyes from telling the truth
to all, maintain the same
benevolent façade they do,
never letting it fall for
a minute, never let that
look between the look
ever reveal more than you
want it to reveal, deny
any hint of discomfort,
hostility, remember that
the people you deal with
have the most fragile
and malleable of psyches,
let the strain flow out
of your fingertips, let
your eyes fix on an
object not connected to
anyone, relax, relax, enjoy.

Untitled

it is frightening
waking up to yourself
numb, disconnected
pacing dream goals
that the world won't let you touch
and that others-feeling
the sense of need
shifting itself
from below the belt
to completely gone

Untitled

We glance at each other
in the middle of nothing nowhere
and your gaze asks me to
say something, to offer
some kind of statement
that can move things forward
but I have nothing prepared
that I can say, nothing I can tell
you, I don't know what you
want from me, and the glance
adds up to nothing but
I'm sorry

Advice

tangible break patterns in solitude sky:
I can only advise what I know,
and what I know is little, little
and fruitless

I can tell you some things I think,
but as far as long-term concerns,
I am only really sure that it is
always her decision and it is
always her regret

if you need anything more from me
I will be waiting for life to happen
because as Rilke says:
let life happen to you
because life is in the right
always

The First Nervous Breakdown

Ceremonies and processions
floating feet on grass in a stampede
of men and women in brown capes and square hats
and humidity of peach and lavender
A life of childish ambition at its logical end

My beautiful ladies! My muses!
I think of calling to all of you
to ask you what I need to do with myself
but the answer is right in front of me:
march onward, frail little warrior,
for if the foot soldiers do not get you,
the horsemen certainly will

Untitled

It just set in,
at the lowest moment I stood:
I cannot have you
and the closest I can get
is a pencil sketch I drew, of you,
from a photograph I found lying in a well
stained with moss and soaked with dark water
but I can still see through the outline
and into your face for relief

Untitled

In stupor of love fantasies
and night steam
I flow like vagabond piss
down the dry corridors
(arousing looks of confusion
and unconscious anger)
but there is no way
to turn back waste into drink
or make living matter
less pungent

A Snake in June

Can you see my cheeks flair and expand?
My eyes become a pearly glint?
I had my rattle removed at an early age,
for I felt it was too easy a warning sign.
I strive for the impulsive and
I strain for the expulsion
when my venom is in reserve

A Duet for Cannibals

We both step left,
We both step right,
keeping with the slow
orchestral sound
and it is only when
the music stops do
We stop and consume each other,
fangs on fangs and
nails on skin

Absolution

I think it's about time
to put this one to rest
I am finished arguing my part
and standing up for my ideals
so I can only stand aside
and let your false stance blaze on
allowing you to believe you won
so that the two of us can start,
once more,
from scratch

Untitled

"Fornication's overrated"
sang the choir boys
while they masturbated

Alone We Can Do Nothing Together

2003

Dedicated to the memory of Martin Kippenberger

"Kiss any girl you please! If there's still time! Here's to you! If you live! The rest'll come all by itself! Happiness, health, grace and fun! Don't worry too much about me! set your little heart going!"

- Louis-Ferdinand Céline, *Guignol's Band*

Morning Routine

I flex the curve of learning
snatching cherries from the tree
but those daily cups of coffee
ruined all the taste for me

Untitled

i see how it will be
now, when love is in bloom,
and my heart is set on knowing;
a force, clenched inside my head
is going to tamper with me,
a voice conjured by you
and you alone
it is going to sadden me
and burden me
and i cannot wait for it to stop

Untitled

No, sorry, life is not like that
or like anything else you mentioned
at least according to my travels
or the tales I've heard and retained

to me it is a roving tragedy
containing fear and unbridled corruption
and has everything to do with disguise
for what are we but the clothes we wear?

I've taken the musings of minstrels,
lately, with a pinch of delicacy
realizing I've been there before, mentally,
while jogging in middle-class Paradise

Untitled

not everyone is beautiful
and not everyone is talented
not everyone is successful
and not everyone is lucky
not everyone is a winner
and not everyone is needed
not everyone is a blessing
and not everyone deserves love

though when you lack those little things,
and recognize that you do,
you look around to those near you,
and imagine you are the only one
but fear not, and want not, and need not,
for everything in your fragile hands
is exactly as it should be
or so we all need to believe

A Letter to the Son I'll Never Have

things can never be planned
and this is one flaw for which I am sorry
it never did materialize
although it was my intention to make it work

what was done was beyond my reach
and I certainly never planned it
and I can't tell you how fantastic it would have been
to spend time talking to and advising you

movements pushed me forward
to a breaching contractual mess
and these chemicals simply never clicked
because science is not an art
and love is not a science

bench parks could have been discussion tables
and the kitchen could have been Congress
the back room could have been yours to use
in any fruitful manner you wished

what remains is an alternate journey
one that has been given to me
you shall remain in infinity or be given away
to those that truly deserve you
and grant you the freedom you need like I need:
the kind we could have shared together

Nobody Helps Anybody

to you i have shown mercy
but in no usual way
the kindness is all hidden
and behind hard work is play
i think of your best interests
while defiling your good name
i realize you don't like it
but it's the way i play the game

Atlantic City

the honeymoon has been over
the last thirty plus years
and the bridesmaid has gained weight
and the groom is remarried
the vagrants are many
on the rotting boardwalk
and not even Mr. Trump himself
can turn everything around

the future is coming
but first goes the slums
and then all the dealers
and their streetwise corruption
take care of the politics
and rebuild the rubble
you can certainly do better
for the ocean deserves more

Playing Checkers on Saturday Night

your numbers and statistics and logic
are a little questionable, my Princess,
but I think highly of you all the same
your double-talk and plain-English
highlight certain laconic
but still cherishable traits
that I did not notice before
(but would have loved to find)
paintings and alcohol and checkers
fail to thrill the spirits inside you,
and you'll always need something more
and separately we shall seek out
the wit of writing
and the sensation of flesh on flesh:
you through the allure of male sensuality
and I through the pleasure of memory

Young Man's Lament

Mom's such a sick fuck
You probably should know
and Dad is no better
I'm letting you know
My brother's a suitcase
and sis is a trollop
they're no good for being
so I'll just stay alone

Testament

testament, testimony
fragranced nights persist
but thought still seems an issue
as it
shuttles to sideways
riddles plans
and scrambles the words
I meant to say

The City of Sin in the Summer of Love

<u>Departure</u>

during every early morning
I shamefully want to die
but thirty minutes pass
and my reason's presence returns

I spot four crisp ladies
finding shelter in Philadelphia
only to fly back to Nairobi
via an airport afraid to breathe

'American families doing better'
the tickertape announces
over and over, syncopating
while lapse women with caked makeup
offer orange juice diluted with ice
to the ungrateful in transit

Arrival

the debauched landscape
is divided by a median
into slum and plastic gem
if you thought Walt constructed
the most perfect scam
his brilliance has been one-upped

foreign beds and greased poles
become bargaining tables
in nights of frivolity, extroversion
but it has all the fervor
of a legitimate transaction
(like leasing an El Dorado)
and pleasure is just another commodity

Experience

children of fourteen blink slowly
within the palace of sequence
uncomfortable with their parents' impatience
and flushed with heat of desert

a two-toothed man with stubble
will ask if you would like ecstasy
but tell him you're already ecstatic
to make him go away

it's the prom you never went to:
a warm, well-presented buffet
filled with treats and goodies
but the delectables are inedible
since they all bear waxed coating

Closure

if thoughts are in a vacuum
and their recurrence inevitable
the same maneuver will be initiated
again and again and again
to provide many a soulless utopia
and sour the seeds of conquest

should I ever return
I will keep in mind your faults
and be prepared for the late nights,
and the lost girls of Déjà Vu
(who so willingly accepted my voyeurism)
and the fake tickets and porn warriors,
and the Vicodin and the crippled beggars
but for now it is goodbye beautiful summer
as well as goodbye wicked fuckers forever

Seats 24 A-B-C

you spent some time in Hong Kong
before departing for Germany
you live inside Nevada
but commute sans friends to Jersey
you slept on a bench in Marseille
and borrowed change from giving London
you jumped around in Boca
but never wandered to Atlanta

you stretched out due to vacancy
but never looked across at me
to relay the details of these stories
and let me remember them for free
you told the broad from nowhere
who could hardly give a damn
she forgot them in a minute
which was probably your plan

Untitled

Oh! Paths and journey!
The automobile provides your guidance
like the satyr with a boarding pass
or the soldier and his cardboard chariot
across the awkward landscape
of haunted, glorious America.

The Last Stop West

the mood still hasn't changed
and the geography is still the same
and the people are still brutal
in their Armani or Prada or Givenchy
with their Davidoffs trailing along
there isn't any free water or nickel coffee
and I am still frighteningly alive
but there's grace and repose in knowing
that at least it is not yesterday

Untitled

I have seen the edge
of human thought
and reconciled the love
of peace, tranquility
for the lust for depravity

Capitalism in Tijuana

if money can do it
consider it done
by anyone standing idle
in the Mexican sun

the mules live with peasants
and the peasants can't sleep
and their goods are all worthless
but luckily they're cheap

grandma begs for dollars
and granddaughter does too
even though she's a toddler
a few quarters will do

shame is in shortage
and pride's hit a wall
tourism's the bright spot
in this drab shopping mall

Piece I

chrome-stained leaves
that drift off the trees
gather and please
my prostrated knees

Untitled

porous and open,
(yet not so)
and seemingly hollow -
he finds the strands
and tugs them firmly
with intent
and they give
but not to the degree
one would ask them to

Desire (Part I)

the only thrill still present
in those two aging spirits
the Mother and Father in America
comes through the sexual lives
of their children, well into puberty
all hormonally enraged and confused
and pressured to make a move

Father sees himself in the cocksure son
while allowing his libido the last stretch
of duty-free screwing
(or seeing in his daughter's friends
girlfriends of his youth)
and Mom becomes protective,
mending the tear in her own womb
while reliving past lusts
and the mistakes she remembers making

Desire (Part II)

the sexualization of culture
has brought about a drought
that forms inside the bedroom
and generates self-doubt

for lust has been subsided
by muted apathy
all the billboards feature fucking
for the frilly selling spree

there's signs and symbols urging
and there's children selling too
regardless of things like morals
or societal taboo

passion has been mopped up
and the pavements have gone dry
arousing thoughts aren't working
though you certainly can try

A Night Out

we dress like urban losers
and we act like randy fools
we talk a wicked battle
and attended pricey schools
but we're no better off than you are
and your luxurious enterprise
our intentions are mostly honest
and our frowns merely disguise

Request

disease strike me not
illness plague me not
injury find me not
for I err on the side of caution

instantaneous elimination would be far gentler
and also more preferred
over the more egregious methods
of your dealing suffering to people

(think: swift, silent, instant)

Piece II

moribund highs
and blind-siding lows
hinder the progress
on the way to the throne

Untitled

cruel and barbaric,
it sings to the common crowd
with an eye for vengeance
and an ear for lies
such is the nature of hypocrisy
and the eagerness for revolt

Dreaming

the dreams are nursed in darkness,
Genet writes from tiny cell
reaching to the strangers
from his own private hell
the walls provide no answers
as the conscious heart expires
the worms await the phantoms
and the bodies find their fires

Untitled

Taste!
The foe bubbles up my esophagus
and yearns to see her cup again,
that resting spot in glass,
but I insist the foam remains
lest I become too upset
or in the mood to purge

Advice

look forward to nothing
and be sure to expect even less
don't become eager or excited
don't wait for things to work
never idolize anyone equal to you
but listen for the words between the words
embrace nothing but this very moment
give others the chance to do the same
and pity them when they cannot

The Second Nervous Breakdown

it started on the downswing
and ended on the upswing
following the deserted presentation
and the sandstorms of aggression

beckoned for the comforts of childhood
without solace in tomorrow
sat with fear as the clowns beside me
experimented with masochism and sickness

crippled and shaking before religious icons
begging for assistance and pity,
and filled with fear of losing it all again,
the tremor in the throat that forbids food,
the clot in the head that stops movement,
and the double vision, so unexpected,
all coming back to haunt and disturb

my right arm trembles still
although the war's reached an impasse
and my knees are weak from stumbling
though my heart is still a-flutter
I've found that blind acceptance is still best,
for denial, it is indeed true,
gets you through the final act.

Untitled

clock ticks like a fever-demon
find husband build house make baby
and the wedding columns in the paper
are a daily slap in the face
but cherish your free time
and do not rush into a struggle
celibacy is a delicacy
and canines make loving friends

Moment I

admirable, in a way,
how you absorb all my distortions
pushed inside of you and
coated with the layers of excess
I know you will want to believe

admirable, truly,
how far you will go to delude yourself
into thinking I am who I play
and not some different, dissimilar
monstrosity, deriving pleasure
from deceiving you.

Moment II

I could be inches from death,
from leaving you for eternity,
and I will never stop telling you
you were the only one, and
that I cared for only you,
because with the end I take it all
with me, and leave you with the
piece I manufactured
for you to hold within you
for the rest of your days

(and it will come out like
the sweetest of songs,
me being caught up
in the moment
and playing the role
I must)

Moment III

for the rest,
the same truth is coming,
and without sadness or remorse
I tell you all is fine,
that I feel splendid,
all the while waiting for you
to leave me,
so I never had to look at you
or anyone like you
and pleased with that kind of freedom

Untitled

it's all in your head
as a matter of fact
the price of misgivings
and the ink on the pact
the gold's kept in storage
and the lies in the shed
you'll make the concessions
moments after you're dead

Marathon

if all is still knowing
and the answer is dim
find hope, my new comrade
for we are not ahead of you
but shoulder to shoulder
in stride
looking forward
and never sideways

Conclusion

I do not know much
but realize this:
we are but flashing moments,
  flittering
  fluttering
  dazzling
  purposeless
  gone.

The K.E.N.O! Pamphlet

2003

"The historic ascent of humanity, taken as a whole, may be summarized as a succession of victories of consciousness over blind forces - in nature, in society, in man himself."

- Leon Trotsky

Here Are The Young Savages
(The Organization)

I.

the serpentine path which was theirs to follow
was granted by divine wisdom
a siren from the mystical One
gracing them with breath at the precise time
that was their want and angelic call
the Young Savages formed from similar organs
meeting in entangled twists
the semen and sweat glistened as they will forever
to replicate and expend DNA
the DNA flowing from one to another
and prompting the future of the illusion

II.

The Young Savages look young and healthy and full of
potential, their faces showing concern and interest,
their heads packed with information and new ideas,
their pockets empty but eager to be filled.

III.

The Young Savages tell you that the Old Regime
is Outdated, that those before them are Fools, that
Their Way is better, that they want to Better Mankind
and the Cost of Daily Living

IV.

The Young Savages use considerable sway to force their
way into Politics, Entertainment, Corporate Offices
and make everyone pay attention,
because as Youth Culture will tell you,
everyone loves Youth Culture
and the Promise They Carry For a
Better Tomorrow

V.

The Young Savages open the floodgates
(once they've been given the key)
and at first are free to show kindness and generosity
to those that elevated them to the level of Gods,
gracious and accepting and humble and sweet,
they kiss the mouths of progress
and wipe the tears of surrender
off the faces of the fallen
who are executed in back alleys
or locked away in cramped rooms

VI.

The Young Savages make good on their promises
in the beginning, picking up the crippled
and shoveling money to the Right People at the
Right Time counting on the Right Decisions
and giving the Right Answers,
and for a while All is Calm and All is Prosperous

VII.

But like the Empires of the Past, the Young Savages
will grow older, and with age, comes the Timeless
Ideas of Old, and with The Old Ideas comes the Old
Problems, growing callous and indifferent, no longer
full of promise and strong ideas, exhausted and bankrupt
in every possible way, but fearing the long-standing
grip on all-elusive Power, so therefore the Dictatorship
is formed to eliminate dissent

VIII.

And eventually the Former Young Savages are being
challenged by the New Young Savages, original
and fresh faced, eager to upset the balance and
take their place in the elite, which disgusts the Old
Savages, the Despotic Savages, the Savages who have covered
up the Secret Executions and the Secret Dossiers
and Secret Operations to Oppress, Convict, Assassinate,
Silence and Imprison

IX.

The battle ensues, and from the Battle, Youth wins,
The New Young Savages conquer the Old Savages, frail
and fragile as they are, and take their positions at the
apex of the pyramid, grateful to those who stood by
them and acted as the backs and feet to step on and
over, claiming responsibility for the Quest for Progress
and Ecstatic over eliminating the Old Savages and their
Sinister Regime

X.

And so the New Young Savages make good on their promises
in the beginning, picking up the crippled
and shoveling money to the Right People at the
Right Time counting on the Right Decisions
and giving the Right Answers,
and for a while All is Calm and All is Prosperous

But like the Empires of the Past ...

K.E.N.O!
(The Doctrine)

"… [H]atred strikes me as one of the few signs of life remaining in the world. This is another thing about the world which is upside-down: all the friendly and likable people seem dead to me; only the haters seem alive."

- Walker Percy, *The Moviegoer*

A.

Pain is a goldmine and love is a travesty
domination rules the cruel like the mantle
in the hands of past Kings,
moving past the years of the uncivilized
but never making any progress -
Stalin may have loved it and
Nietzsche may not have been far behind -
because the destitute continue running the asylum
and the people we're producing in
the factories beneath our buildings
are not much of an improvement
over the previous models

B.

Intelligence seems to be something
too much to ask for,
as is kindness and compassion and
warmth and tenderness,
the barbaric continue trolling the alleys of progress
and the powerless attempt to lord over the frail,
and the frail will always be that way,
the stepping stones for the forward minded
but empty-headed,
knowing that no one gets anywhere
in their hurry to win the championship

C.

Rejection comes quickly to the sad souls,
the incompetent and the lonely,
the vain and the restless,
the tempted and the betrayed,
in a single instance of time,
fleeting moving cavorting aerodynamically,
the personal damage so much so that
recovery is neither immediate
nor everlasting

D.

The only return for the inflicted injury
is a massive counterstrike
a lashing of the oppressed and the depressed
a swipe at the faceless oppressor,
willing to take risks and willing to cause injuries,
even the loss of the self,
of the potential for the ego-ideal,
desperate to start the revolution
and to compensate for the humiliation

E.

K.E.N.O! demands change and alteration!
K.E.N.O! demands the deaths of the oppressive!
K.E.N.O! demands the death of capitalism!
K.E.N.O! will reinstate the gas ovens!
K.E.N.O! insists on the shallow suffering!
K.E.N.O! realizes that misery must be universal!
K.E.N.O! understands that the days of millions are wasted!

F.

K.E.N.O! is tired of racism!
K.E.N.O! is tired of prejudice!
K.E.N.O! does not tolerate the power-hungry!
K.E.N.O! wants to defend the silenced!
K.E.N.O! believes in progress, however
K.E.N.O! questions the motives of mankind!

G.

K.E.N.O! loves the Australians!
K.E.N.O! loves the Canadians!
K.E.N.O! loves the open-minded! however
K.E.N.O! cannot fathom how things went so wrong!
K.E.N.O! is against all religious practices!
K.E.N.O! cannot comprehend ignorance!
K.E.N.O! cannot stand squalor!
K.E.N.O! is sickened by the present conditions!
K.E.N.O! does not find itself amusing!
K.E.N.O! is sickened by mass ignorance!
K.E.N.O! demands harmony!
but since harmony cannot be demanded
K.E.N.O! therefore demands total elimination!

H.

human waste, one imagines, flows from purgatory;
if such a sanctum exists it isn't for me to say
if there's anything left to do for the false saints
and the mad prophets with their wooden canes and flasks,
it's the dream for lacerated tongues and the end of language,
for the limits of our reality are the limits of our speech.
and the end of speech signifies the end of reality

I.

K.E.N.O! is Just for everyone
and yet Just for no one at all.

The Engineer
(The Implementation)

The men and women in cramped warehouses
build bridges! and roads! automation!
circuits! factories! the way of progress!

6:15

wake up, stare at the alarm clock playing knights in
white satin, disc jockeys laughing in the background
room cold, left side of body hurts slightly, room smells
like perfume and sweat, not wearing pajama bottoms
need to wash pillow that is currently hugging my head

6:40

wander into bathroom covered with blanket, shower to
heat up use dial to lather and denorex to de-flake,
dry hair, gel hair, brush, deodorant, visine, shave, towel
off, place on clothing, not thinking all that clearly
visions roam wildly like that of lions darting through
the crest

7:10

breakfast most important meal said by someone who
woke up at noon and enjoyed sunshine and wealth
with his coffee, never worked in today's conditions,
I take a muffin from the basket downstairs
and get my heavily sugared coffee from the drive-by
stand (those people are nice) on the way

8:20

saunter past fat man whose face sags and whose
neck is virtually nonexistent we don't say anything
to each other and I privately hope he has a heart
attack the instant he walks past me and clears out
of my sight and he may very well have but
I refuse to turn around to check

9:00

meeting scheduled by someone I never met before
about progress on million dollar project everyone
jacks off to and also worries about I sit next to
a sad sack old bastard who when he retires will
begin collecting toy trains and I laugh at the thought
while Miguel, two seats down, has fallen asleep
and no one dares to wake him because he's
not American and this scares H.R.

10:40

break from meeting I get coffee some woman from
the company we're dealing with is trying to flirt
with me and I'm not sure why I'm paying attention
to her and I think up a list of insults to say to her
and chuckle in the middle of something she has
to say that isn't funny and she gives me this
strange look I wonder if her asshole is still a virgin,
since all virgins are assholes

11:30

I am growing tired early and tear into a frosted apple pie
I fear my eyesight may begin to deteriorate from
staring at my monitor typing if/then statements
and writing headers and compiling code and
I develop an erection thinking about the janitor
girl who takes my garbage that is very nice
to me but she is only a janitor and that is unacceptable

12:00

full from pie and coffee and jittery I take off my shoes
and walk into the bathroom to defecate and scald my hands
when I go back to my desk Pete is waiting and
he's handing me papers and I tell him it's my lunch
but he doesn't much care one time I went to Pete's
house and he had one table and a television set
and a bed and nothing else, he's hoarding his money
like an asshat and he thinks I care about what he's
handing me and I take it from him and set it someplace
I don't have to look at it

1:30

three cups of coffee later and I'm still trying to order
some part from a distributor in what can only be
Taipei because he understands nothing and I
speak into the receiver as slowly as I can and I think about the
comic panel I saw in the New Yorker that had
a nursery of little children playing with blocks
and writing the alphabet on the chalk board and
crying over spilled milk and underneath the
caption read "how engineers look at everyone else"

2:15

I generate this bizarre fantasy in my mind about
drugging Zoë in Accounting and covering her
entire body with burlap and crawling naked over her
so that my face is right above her face and then
prying her right eye open and licking it and this
thought arouses me for a minute but I realize when
the moment passes its effectiveness, too, will
pass and later on I will think it merely disturbing

3:00

Mike's telling me all about his wife and he's
come to my cubicle and I can't seem to get rid
of him, how cute she is how wonderful she can
be and I remind him that I was at the wedding but
I secretly find her repulsive and Mike repulsive
and I have a secret bet with Craig as to when they'll
split up and I'm pretty sure it will be sooner than later

3:50

I pride myself in taking as much as possible from the
Honesty Box without putting in change, and I realize
the guilt from the taking without paying is supposed
to affect everyone but it really bothers no one, at least
no one I spend my days with and someone is always
trying to leave notes to put in X dollars but we all find
this amusing

4:10

I urinate all over the men's room floor and then masturbate to the mental image of the janitor girl coming in later to mop it up and I swear she's no older than 25 and I feel this tremendous pity for her and for some reason I imagine she can recognize the smell of the piss on the floor (as I've done this before) and how she touches herself while she mops it up and this allows for the release and only afterwards does it not make sense but that's the way the orgasm functions, I suppose

4:45

the compiler errors mount up on this endless thing I've been working on all afternoon and I've broken out the manuals to figure it the hell out and I have minimal luck and my headache is resurfacing right above my right eye and it's throbbing and I'm stomaching tylenol and mylanta simultaneously

5:30

technically my day was over at 5:00 but something isn't
finished and someone called an impromptu meeting
and I'm back in the same seat in the conference center
and it's freezing cold in here and my hands are tucked
under my pants and Miguel isn't here and Pete is actually
trying to be furious and calm at the same time and I find
myself nodding while thinking about how large the window
panel behind him is in inches and then centimeters

6:15

smoke rises from Miguel's cubicle and everyone rushes
over to see if he burned himself and if he's okay but privately
everyone is hoping he electrocuted himself by jerry rigging the
wiring in his cubicle and he's trying to solder this piece
together and it isn't working out right but we all give him
encouragement and leave him be promptly disappointed at the
non-disaster meanwhile I stare at the clock and want to leave
but everyone else is still plugging so I can't sneak away
and I don't know how long my Walter Mittyesque flights of
fancy can keep me amused and entertained

7:30

I'm desperately hungry and on the treadmill at the Gold's Gym
to work off as many calories as possible and I'm still getting
pudgy and I bawl while I'm on it though no one
notices, the sweat and the tears and my facial expression
soaked and runny and I imagine I'm running from something,
something following me, and my legs go and go
and no one hears me yelping because they're all wired into
their headphones

7:45

I run into an old High School classmate outside and she's
quite heavy and when she asks what's going on I tell her
everything with the glossiest sheen and maximum smugness
and I sense a bit of hostility in how she cuts me short and
this amuses me on the drive home and this time I'm laughing
and god this really made my day, she's in retail but
wants to be an dancer and I'm laughing so hard I drown out
the hockey commentators on the radio

9:00

after two scotches and a bowl of mashed potatoes and my
left-over steak sandwich from a few days ago I watch TV
and the images glaze over me and the channel surfing
is completely hypnotic and the phone's ringing but let
them think I'm busy and I'm covered in several blankets
snuggled up like the most content animal you can possibly
imagine and I remember how Gene told me that when he
was in Greece all you had to do was turn on the TV and
there was CNN, there was America, wherever you went

10:30

I stomp heavily upstairs and brush my teeth and slide
into bed and thoughts of something I forgot to finish
up form my head and all I can think about in the
darkness is this project, this objective, and I toss
and turn and don't know why it's bothering me since
I honestly don't care, but my mind cares, and the fear
that begins to erupt is the kind I felt on Sunday nights
and was explaining to my mother how I wished the weekend
would go on like it did with no interruption and
she told me that no, education is so important for you
it's so important you go to school in the morning and
that you be smart and better and she was right,
at least, in principle.

For Natalie and Natalie and Natalie

2006

For Natalie

Timely Camaraderie

Nat Cat it's Matt Cat good afternoon tiny gal
it isn't so often we visit or fondle or think,
we lived in memories of moment
and the moment was not so much time
as space improper

it's as if seconds we spent within
the same vicinity, that gauzy yellow fortress,
were but a motion blur,
like faces and bodies disintegrated into streaks
of white and gray, flesh distorted by a
Neuromachine! those lamentable four years!

I fear this is my own interpretation, and
I lay on my bed with sickened pit in my
abdomen, trying so hard to recall
conversations we had and the classes we took and
the air we breathed for I realize now that we
had much in common and much to accomplish

for instance, I remember a young you
spoke with me while we stood in line -
any line - and when the line dried up we
separated but I felt rejuvenated, the way a friend
consoles and imparts and thinks of your best
intentions, having not arrived in said line so
assured and so pleased

It was but ten years ago - this being the tenth
anniversary (my God are we decaying! the
fire between the toes reminds me of the
fact!), but it feels foreign and haunting, like

random daydreams I have for my current job,
a day job, with sunshine telling me to look up
and look sharp

Should you ask if I'd like to return to those days,
however, I cannot help but say no,
for the experience is lived and the past is safe

Distance

I believe I was intimidated
by your worldliness and Life Knowledge,
my naivety having met its match.
My heart was tied to another in the room -
a kinky-haired cheerleader with freckles
and a smile to kill your family for (so it
was, so it was) - and somehow I
never took you seriously: fine as friend,
chat companion a blessing and a half
but lover improbable

Experience

I pray you didn't look back
in disappointment or disgust -
it goes without saying that
we need to keep apologizing
for the mistakes of our younger selves,
though keeping hold over our older selves
is essential, Nat Cat, and we've both lost
touch with ourselves - I've drifted and
wandered after leaving the college nest,
accumulating experience and practiced
being a student of life but retaining the mindset
of an immortal 21-year-old,
furious and virulent,
immature and loathsome,
alone and lonely

I travel like a journalist with a headache
across the seas when not sipping dark rum
in the Caribbean or sipping dark coffee
in Brussels with fellow divas in heat
I have no attachments or direction,
elegantly wasted and
elegantly wasted and
elegantly wasted,
avoiding work and
drinking tea and
crying over the slightest thing

I read about you in the local news rag,
Nat Cat, which has me concerned.
The headline was not empowering,
the content considerably less so.

You abandoned your child in Easton,
Nat Cat, you were arrested with crack,
Nat Cat, the officers took no pity,
Nat Cat, but the judge was understanding.
I've seen moving pictures
about being inelegantly wasted,
Nat Cat, but never pictured you.

Redemption

It's tempting to think we could have
somehow saved each other,
your inelegance and my faux-elegance
negating each other, steady on the path to courtship.
I don't believe I ever saw the Real You
(nor you the Real I!)
or maybe it was my youth that prevented it -
I still thought no one committed serious crimes
or poisoned their blood or crumbled into a million
tiny pieces like Frey pretended he did (a lie! a lie!)

A semi-stable home life is a marvelous invention
for a child: it produces fight or flight,
Jamesian as that might be

But Nat Cat, nonetheless, I do hope for your safety.
Nat Cat, be a mother to someone.
Nat Cat, be someone to love.

... and Natalie ...

One

you were so professional
professional as one could ever hope to be
closer to fame and excellence
than a preteen could be trained
not possessing the most monumental of talent
but skilled enough and charming enough
to sleep comfortably at night

Two

let me ask you this:
do beautiful girls take milligrams of pleasure?
do they stare into puddles and
praise their face and fate?
do they look for kings
among the daisies in the morass,
using their freshly painted nails to
pry apart the asphalt on Rodeo?

Three

does psychology help you
sort out your demons, organizing
and sorting and compiling lists and
traits of potential and shiftlessness?

are boys (or girls?) more difficult to pick
than scripts bound and delivered?
are career decisions more tangible
than love decisions? are my questions
befitting a queen?

we saw each other once, in a
cardboard box with Anna Paquin inside,
and the glances amounted to null - I
become enamored with your glorious
little frame (knowing you were out of
touch, literally, physically, spiritually)
though still of the age where dreaming
befitted a bum such as myself

'the girl's too much' the boys agreed,
and the decision stood

Four

if you could change it all, would you?
were your high school days gloomy or bright?
if you didn't have those looks or that luck?
would you be slumped in a desk, head
in hands, wondering why the boys don't like you?
would it be any different than it is now?

Five

if you could offer advice to the Girls of Today,
would it mean anything to them?
could you mean anything?
are you closer to fulfilling Maslow's Hierarchy,
with all the slots filled and check marked?
when young girls look up to you,
do you look down at them?
or do you look them right in the eye
and say you understand,
having searched for your own time
and your own place, with the pomegranate
stains on your fingers and the Wailing Wall
but an ocean away?

... and Natalie.

Summertime Blues

there is no cure for
the death of youth
you can beat it to the punch
but then you're just a tragedy,
pitied and unfulfilled,
decaying before your bones had
time to naturally erode,
a legend if you gave hint
of your potential legend,
otherwise but a memory to few,
a waste of time to others, a
footnote to a footnote to a
footnote

as we sat in the heat
and you continuously passed
out and reawakened (while I watched you),
I can't help but feel we were both
exhausted then, not simply physically
but psychically, our souls frail and weary
and in need of sleep,
or even perhaps small gestures, like automatic fans
aimed at our prostrate bodies,
with kisses on our sweet, soaked foreheads
and tissues to wipe the love off our stomachs

Competition

I sense where your throes lie:
a sibling that can do no wrong
and a family that neglects you
and classmates that never understood,
stuck in the fringes, like myself or
my old friend Nat Cat, seeking acceptance
like Ms. Nat Paramour, but remaining your
own Nat, placeless and wild, Bohemian
and neurotic, shifty and edgy

living like a nomad isn't a dream
parents conjure for their fragile kin,
parents thrive on buzzwords like *safety*
and *family*, and I'm of the age now
to tell you that the on-the-roaders are
dead, and that there are coffee shops
where Woodstock stood, and the
drive from the Hotlantic to the Pacific
is long, long, long, long without music
and patience; don't be afraid to come
back with tail wrapped around neck
or infant in the cradle

Brotherhood and Sisterhood

it's a hard lesson to learn when
your friends walk away from you,
for I too know the feeling,
that History you accumulated
over the years and years suddenly dust,
as the interests and experiences
that were built and examined
are now ruined and formless,
as if they never happened at all,

why bother, you ask yourself,
but why bother to ask yourself?

Independence Gained

how much money do you need
to make it on your own?
you're wearing out so fast so fast
with jobs that link both day and night
I can't fault your work ethic,
but you are scattershot and lost -
there's no peace for you in the food of home,
in the cold of Ireland, of the noise in your
basement - it's all very clear, so translucent
and pure, and imprinted on the soles
of your bare, blackened feet

Endearment (1)

It may not mean much to you now,
but my smiles are and will be genuine
and my intentions are and will be sincere -
it's like I'm begging for friendship, but
I'm not so distant - if distance is the equality
of emotional duress - and I lament to report that
the more I'm away the more irritable I've gotten,
like those creeping sores on the side of the torso
from curling in a corner
or refusing to leave the bedside

do you feel the same?
or would that say too much about you?

Endearment (2)

I want to share a cup of coffee with
you, Brave Nat, and the Nat Cat and the Ms. Nat
in the mostly barren fields in N.Y. state
where Hendrix discovered fire and music
mix, I want to go to a concert with you
and the Nat Cat and the Ms. Nat and
smell the smoke and feel the noise in
my chest wall, in my collapsible lung.
I want a round table on a tattered blanket,
not to be laughed at but real,
a union of the three snakes,
a meeting of the similarities and
differences

Endearment (3)

I run my fingertips over the side walls
your dirty hair stuck to, climb the chalk
hallways where paint is peeling but
the floors are always waxed, I search
for the Sublime in the asphalt where your
tracks burned lines, I look for fallen
apples near Blowjob Park where you park
and hopefully keep your mouth clean,
I'd pay money, serious money, honest money,
to know exactly where I was
when you began falling apart

Notebook on Anxiety

2018

Dedicated to the memory of Jean-Paul O'Connor

"The order of the world is always right — such is the judgment of God. For God has departed, but he has left his judgment behind, the way the Cheshire Cat left his grin."

- Jean Baudrillard

Untitled

There are many items one can use
to soothe an aching back in the absence of ice
I, for one, have used a frozen filet of fish
a refrigerated bottle of Rolling Rock
a TV dinner box whose content is expired
a poorly sealed bag of unused corn
the chilled plate that once held a peach pie
the steel of a door exposed to the night air
but what works best, in my own experience, is
the disembodied hand of a phantom from afar

A Precursor

When I was born my lips turned blue
you can ask the nurse - she saw it too
amniotic fluid infected my chest
so she wrapped me tight against her breasts
spiking with fever, not sure to exist
unaware that what barely began could soon desist
cords were wrapped around my newborn body
prayers were said by Father in the lobby
Eleven days later, the airways got fixed
Mom recovered too, my pneumonia was nixed
The medical staff likely figured I didn't have long
to survive among many with no shine in their song
And maybe they're right and maybe I'm dreaming
and maybe we shouldn't halt the urge to start screaming

Untitled

All hail to you, the Bastard King!
let's see what newfound trouble you bring
The chalice is poisoned, the table is clear
The altar you're perched on is stained with beer
Let's sit obediently and hear your great speech
and tell us how greatness was within your reach
but the marauders did take it and ride to the night
a mad galloping fury! a nocturnal delight!
Include us in your new elaborate scheme
a blueprint of madness just to keep with the theme
We'll pillage and plunder and incite a fierce brawl
and fail and retreat and try to make sense of it all
then you'll jettison off to find a shiny new crew
bidding us wounded warriors not one fair adieu

Untitled

"Fight or flight": I learned about it as an undergrad
you're given the example of a bear in the woods
so with the massive animal you have two choices:
you run from it (but it's faster so it can catch you)
you duke up with it (but it's stronger so it can kill you)
I'm not sure how that's remotely helpful
and I would prefer a third, more sensible option:
lay out a checkered blanket, put lots of snacks on it
a turkey platter, some kalamata olives, bruschetta toasts
perhaps a cold bottle of Chablis you had soaking in the creek
and have a discussion with the irate creature,
share your feelings and aspirations, a friendly cuddle
then wouldn't all things be in alignment after all?

Regarding Order and Symmetry

I.

Alarm goes off, time to make the bed
with the corners perfectly tucked
and the pillows stacked neatly
check the phone, purge the spam e-mails
Outside, cigarette number one gets lit
and my arms gets checked for strange marks
or rashes. the legs get examined for creases
Cereal follows a cup of boiling black tea
with only a tablespoon of milk
and half a tablespoon of sugar

II.

Inside, the Market gets looked at
heavy short interest on one of my babies
plummeting a glorious negative 11 percent
The hands get washed with scalding water
my face gets stared at in the bathroom mirror
to see if there are any new lines to fret over
Sometimes the floor of my room accumulates
tiny black specks of fuzz and pieces of plastic
I use a wad of tape to collect what I can
I'm surprised I show up anywhere on time

III.

When I'm wherever I need to be,
my main concern is my level of discomfort
I routinely check my pulse to count the beats
and glance over every aspect of my clothing
Are the pants too wrinkled? Are the laces set?
Does the shirt still fit or did the wash ruin it
The shoes collect the dirt with every single step
so they will need to be boiled when I get home
and my fingernails are probably too long
since they act as reservoirs of the outside grime

IV.

When I'm cutting the grass, which happens a lot,
I get concerned with the lines the tires make
Are they even? Did they leave too many ruts?
Did I absentmindedly run over a tiny rabbit?
Were the snakes squirming beneath me?
I recheck the bottom of my shoes for blades of grass
so I do not track them back into the house
I find myself concerned, for whatever reason,
with the texture of the driveway and pavements
and whether the panels of siding are level

V.

When I'm working on a document,
from the simplest message to a capsule to an essay
everything gets re-written and edited repeatedly
Is this word better than that? Does this make sense?
(My trusted editor is in the other room, knitting socks)
Should I indent this space or that? Does this line sound right?
Is my thesis persuasive? Is my humor coming through?
Am I a smidge too harsh? Or not harsh enough?
(Movies that cost multiple millions don't deserve mercy
for if you wanted that you'd choose a less fickle profession)

VI.

When I'm alone with my thoughts, my fortress gets attention
is the ceiling cracking? is the paint on the wall spread evenly?
what about the collection of clothes in the closet?
the shirts on the right should be on plastic hangers facing right
the pants on the left should be ironed and facing right
the shoes should face forward: sneakers near the bottom
dress shoes (brown and black) near the top, boots above them
I horde handmade clothes like a debutante, a caviar leftist
Made in Italy or Made in France: these are the tags to crave
if you're going to make yourself up, try to buy mystique

VII.

When I'm speaking with others, I'm typically self-conscious
Did I say the wrong thing? Did I tip my hand?
Did I all but tell the other person to piss up a goddamn rope?
Am I yelling? Is my voice too loud? (I feel like I am yelling.)
When I am in a group setting, am I fitting in?
Do I stand out awkwardly like a gawky teenager?
Am I sniffling too much? (I tend to sniffle rapidly.)
Sometimes it's a lot to take, so I exit abruptly
then I worry about bolting, I worry people will find it off-
putting

It's just that disorder is company I prefer not to keep

Untitled

I might be a poseur, but just know that I tried
I might be a fibber, but I know when I lied
I might be a fortress with an emerald spire
I might be a chorus with a glistening lyre
I might be a bad seed giving hope to the lost
I might be a banker with a mind for the cost
I might be an agent of virulent faith
I might be a phantom, a shadow, a wraith
I might be petulant and impulsive, jarringly crude
But I'm the only one that ever tried to make sense out of you

Untitled

keep cover of the hidden hymn you awoke with
for its rhythms are there to hold you
like a tango up on a mountain
or a dirge beneath a lake
keep faithful of your mission,
though it may seem suicidal
like a waltz right off an incline
or the can-can in a war zone
since no one can move the way that you move
and no one knows the lyrics of your heartsong

The Third Pillar

There's a photo of us framed in the basement.
You're holding me in an ochre kitchen
still dressed in your sugar-stained work clothes
and me, a toddler, in a red one-piece.
The look on your face is one of kindness
and that's an expression you never lost
even to the final time I saw you alert on Earth,
confined to a wheelchair and unable to think
and so fitting that I was the last one to hold you
or at least part of you, the vessel you were laid in
as you were carried through a gray, cinematic morning.
My dear friend, I miss you as you said I would
and next we reconvene, allow me into your schedule
for a dinner date: the dessert is on me.

Untitled

I will keep pouring out my heart
so you can keep skipping stones in the puddle
I will keep telling you that I love you
while you laugh at my sincerity
I will keep praying for your wellness
when you damage yourself for chuckles
I will keep trying to protect you
when your violent mouth removes my pride

Untitled

while weeds spring tender
and kisses sting long
inside of your palm print
my wish still belongs

Untitled

age is meaningless for we are infinite
re-spinning and rehashing and repeating
like a sick wheel arcing eternally
where children scream victorious
and the elderly ride on cautiously
it is only a matter of time before
their tenuous roles are reversed
and those waiting in line at the bottom
take their place in the vacant seats

Admonition for an Old Associate (1)

The only question left to ask, then, is this:
Exactly what the hell are you about?
You bounce like a marionette from state to state
Without a fixed identity, like a child released from a closet
After having been locked in there for forty years
One day you're right, one day you're left
A whisper from a truck driver asking for directions
Could redirect your carriage to the Fallen Land
And yet blame, that cursed word, remains at your disposal:
No decision you make is ever yours to own up to
And everyone else is plotting against you
It must be liberating to never be wrong
You must teach me that trick one day

Admonition for an Old Associate (2)

Why is it every time I speak to you
I'm conversing with an expert snake-oil peddler
or a wizened, greasy used car salesman
intent on curing my ails with a vial of nothing
or selling me a jalopy with a rusted bottom
and a bent axle and seats stained with vomit

Everything is a hustle for you
and that must be exhausting, or perhaps not:
maybe the game you spit is ingrained in your soul
or it could be about your parental background
(if we were to get Freudian, which you'd hate)
and the alcoves you call your comfort zone

All your stoolies are in the trade with you
but they grow fewer with each passing year
perhaps the glow of what you call devotion
diminishes for them with the passing seconds
and before they know it they're checking their pockets
to make sure you didn't lift their wallets

Admonition for an Old Associate (3)

I will say yes, it is quite true
I once laid on the couch with you
Or twice, if you count that day in June
After we bathed in chlorine near your room

But you scrambled off and ducked away
That's when your thoughts went all astray
Let's see who else can play my game
The one about seduction, guilt and shame

You told me you couldn't wait to leave
To rip your past right off your sleeve
And by damn you did, without a trace
Grinning as if you escaped the maze

Yet there's too much left that went unsaid
And complex knots in tangled threads
Your wings are wax, your tale's spread thin
The sun is plotting to do you in

Admonition for an Old Associate (4)

You are an unrepentant fraud and a sham
Your gum sticks behind your perfect teeth
Your only light shines in a hovel
Your hollow eyes hide underneath

Does making a fool of a human excite you?
Was I simply a player in your show?
Is there a conscience in your mechanical heart
Or is it too deeply buried below?

Honesty, it's said, is the best policy
But policies are the contracts of the sane
Some people are only as thick as their skin
And their identities confined to their name

Admonition for an Old Associate (5)

Wrap your false honor in a primed canvas
and ship it to your mother's feet
so she can see the good you once had
preserved in amber, safe and concealed
like the American flag on a casket
or a plastic carnation on a cemetery stone

Place your sympathies into a cardboard box
and address them to an absentee father,
himself squeezed into an active Grandfather Clock
but shifty enough to dodge the pendulum swing
May he know of the dredge you summoned
and his eighteen years of investment wasted

Concerning My Own Suffocation

I.

Breathe in. Now breathe out.
Breathe in. Again, breathe out.
Can you feel how natural and free that is?
How normal a sensation that's supposed to be?
Now imagine there's a leather belt wrapped
around your upper torso compressing your lungs
and causing the top of your head to tingle
and your hands to shake voraciously
and your legs to go numb and barely able to support you
and your brain thinking it's deprived of oxygen
and panic settling in and the sensation
that you're about to leave this fragile world
because that, I'm afraid to report, is what happens to me
repeatedly and without fair warning

II.

How it all started? Let's just say I'm not sure
except in the way everything fell apart:
the silent spooks linger in the dank cellar
and tragedy steamrolls in, daring you to stop it
and middle age sets in, even though it's only a number
and the grey hair becomes impossible to pluck
and the Eye of Horus forms in the retina
and the metabolism slows to a steaming crawl
and the bills start mounting even by living frugally
Imagine every little thing going wrong in succession
I know about De Morgan and I know about his Law
but did he ever get rushed to the hospital
on a dehydrating and sunny Friday afternoon
and have multiple vials drawn from his left arm?

III.

I continue to admire the outward cavalier youth
with their disregard for consequences or pain
and sort of flit flat from mortal crater to bomb shelter
wiping the flak and debris off their uniforms
with a quick wipe of the hand and a stroke of the hair
I possessed that indifference, too, but it was so long ago
or maybe I did not, but I was much better at pretending
There's something about the bones decaying
and the enamel rotting and the spine twisting
and the muscles melting and the hair thinning out
to lend that all important gravity to every breath
a collection of *memento mori* built into soft tissue
When once there was alcohol and drugs to have fun
Then there becomes drugs and alcohol to function

IV.

How can one stop worrying when anything can happen
It's like an endless grocery list that can never be filled
you check one item off and another appears at the bottom
one trial gets taken care of and then a new one arises
like multiplying cells in a lab test or bunnies in a bag
Even the celebration from a small victory has no appeal
since defeat is readying itself behind a partition
ready to pounce at the most inopportune moment
and when the onslaught becomes too formidable
the brain reacts unpredictably, sending one into a frenzy
but fighting makes fatigue and that makes us cowards
the temptation to simply flee is all too alluring
please stand in place and wait for the fist to drill you
Just like Miss Fagan sang: *it's easy when you lose*

Untitled

The weight in the abdomen spells the woes of the day
the gurgling swirling agony an obscene alarm clock
the paces through the morning routine search for help
the truth be not forthcoming so only the doubts remain
the opinionated shamans advise deep breaths and slow exhales
the clinic in Rochester suggests chemical concealment
the think tank in Manhattan claims millions are affected
the digital forums remind you that you share suffering
the handful of remedies cure one pain but cause another
the doctors listen slowly but only feign understanding
the situation comes down, ultimately, to patience and
  patience and patience and clarity and patience

Untitled

Heal first, then you may judge
I said to myself, knees on linoleum
face lifted from cold toilet rim
You are in no position to think,
constant pain and tension cloud your judgment
Your bile and blood swirl, your eyes are sunk in
your arms tremble holding your frame in place
And all this not from a single night of wild
but from decades and decades of vice

I have been advised to mime understanding
but all that nodding puts a kink in my neck
this nervousness hastens the speed of clocks
and only attenuates those monthly blues
so sit and shiver and stop thinking of others
stop thinking about their failed decisions
stop dissecting your own character
stop second guessing the heavy feelings
and wait for life to start smiling back

Untitled

Bring me your damaged, your frail,
your psychically infirm yearning
for a quiet realm of peace

Drag their molten corpses down into the
cellar along with their brown bags
and tattered corduroy pants

Take them by the shoulders and shake
them and in shaking them make their pills
dash and scatter on the carpet

Rebuild them in the dwellings and fix
them with nicer things, a bracelet or two
for strength and hand them a bowl of gruel

March them back up the steps into the fields,
whisper a positive prayer into their wrinkled skin
and watch as they fade into the ether

Untitled

who cares about regret, choose failure
who cares about laws, steal love
who cares about time, brew tinctures
who cares about color, print greyscale

who cares about shelter, raise tents
who cares about quiet, craft noise
who cares about sunshine, hug darkness
who cares about money, get candy

Untitled

time began and will cease in a garden
as we stand ready against the pickets
with leaves touching our exposed ankles
and those worm-fed apples kicked aside
the sun-fed rays will blaze and recede
scorching the apex of our temples
we will watch as the horizon bows and bends
exhale as we sink back into the ground
and inhale when we're picked back up again

Untitled

In effect I have been placed
into a state of absolute grace!
May the hands of mystics and wise men
guide me along the path to fulfillment
and hand me the keys to total fortitude
and a locale of loving peace
for the hands of fate have gripped so firmly
I have no other place to breathe
I will wait for the divine to release me
for I anticipate its verdict with piety

Untitled

From the first box we exit
to the last box we're stuffed in
We always end up stinking
of other people's bodies